A SNAKE, A FLOOD, A HIDDEN BABY

BIBLE STORIES FOR CHILDREN

I imagine that some of you think that Bible stories are just what you learn in school and in synagogue. But if so, you are missing out. The Bible contains wonderful stories—about kings and adventures, rivalry among brothers, prophecy and miracles, love and war.

These stories have been passed down from generation to generation for thousands of years. I first heard them from my mother and father, who heard them from their parents. When I grew up I shared them with my children, and now I am sharing them with you, even though you are someone else's children.

This book contains six stories from the Bible. They are about Adam, Eve, and the snake; Noah's Ark and the flood; the Tower of Babel; the angels who visited Abraham and Sarah; Joseph and his brothers; and Moses in the river. I wrote them in language that is slightly more modern, but anyone who wants to read these stories in the Bible—with harder words—is welcome to try. They appear in the very beginning, in the books of Genesis and Exodus.

In addition to the stories, you will also find illustrations by a wonderful Italian artist named Emanuele Luzzati. He wrote and illustrated children's books, built theater sets, and made spectacular animated films.

That's it. I hope you enjoy the stories and illustrations. Regards to your parents.

—MEIR SHALEV

Contents

The Tree of Knowledge

Adam and Eve lived in the Garden of Eden. There were rivers and lakes, birds and beasts, and trees full of fruit. In the middle of the garden stood a beautiful tree called the Tree of Knowledge.

Every day Adam and Eve would take a walk through the garden. They would pass by the Tree of Knowledge and gaze at its fruit. God had said, "You may eat from every tree in the garden, but if you eat from the Tree of Knowledge, you will die."

One day Eve was walking alone in the garden. When she passed by the Tree of Knowledge, she heard a voice whispering from among the branches: "Eve, Eve, pssstpssst . . ."

Eve looked around, and lo and behold, wrapped around the branches of the Tree of Knowledge was a large green snake.

"Come here, don't be scared," the snake said, looking at her with cold eyes.

Eve drew closer, but not too close.

"Do you want to taste the fruit of the Tree of Knowledge?" the snake asked.

"No, no . . . ," Eve stammered. "God told us it was not allowed."

"Ha, ha," laughed the snake. "What do you mean it's not allowed?" He plucked a fruit off the tree, slithered down the thick trunk, and placed it in the grass, next to Eve's feet.

"It's not allowed!" Eve cried.

"Anyone who eats from the Tree of Knowledge will die. That's what God told us."

"What are you talking about?" hissed the snake. "I just picked a fruit. Did anything happen to me? Now I'm going to eat it. Is anything happening to me?" He took a big bite. "Hisss . . . so deliciousss . . ." he said. "It's the most delicious fruit in the garden."

Eve looked at the snake in wonder, because it was true—nothing had happened to the snake.

"Do you know why God does not allow you to eat from the Tree of Knowledge?" the snake asked.

"No," Eve responded. "But the fact that God said so is enough for me."

"I'll tell you why," said the snake. "Because anyone who eats from this fruit will become wise like God. God is afraid that you will become too much like God." And he picked another fruit from the Tree of Knowledge, straightened himself up, and handed it to Eve.

"Would you like a taste?"

Eve felt as if her whole body was trembling. "I just want to touch it," she said, holding out her hand and touching the fruit with her fingertips. Then she took hold of it with her entire hand and brought it to her mouth.

"Yesss . . . yesss . . . ," the snake hissed and drew closer until she could feel his cold skin.

Eve closed her eyes and bit into the fruit, chewing and then swallowing slowly. Nothing terrible happened to her. But when she opened her eyes and saw the snake looking at her again, she felt uneasy, and she hid behind the thick trunk.

"Take one for your husband, too," the snake offered. He leapt down into the high grasses and disappeared.

Eve picked a few more fruits off the tree and brought them to Adam. Adam was alarmed. "You picked fruit from the Tree of Knowledge?" he yelled.

"It wasn't me. It was the snake," Eve responded. "He told me to do it."

"And you ate from it as well?" Adam asked.

"He ate from it, too," Eve responded. "And nothing happened to us. You should try it; it's so delicious."

Adam tasted the fruit, and the two of them looked at each other, blushed, and then burst out laughing.

"Why are you walking around naked?" Eve asked. "You can see everything."

"And why are you walking around naked?" Adam laughed.

"Aren't you embarrassed?"

There were no clothing stores in the Garden of Eden. So Adam and Eve sewed wide sashes out of leaves and wore them over their bodies. When they heard God's voice, they grew frightened and hid.

"Adam!" God called. "Adam! Where are you?"

"There's no one here . . . ," Adam called from among the trees.

"Ahh," said God. "Here you are. Why are you

hiding, and what are these leaves you're wearing?"

"They're just leaves," Adam answered. "It's not appropriate to walk around naked all day. What if someone comes to visit?"

"Who told you that you ought to be embarrassed?" God said angrily. "Did you eat a fruit from the Tree of Knowledge?"

"Eve gave it to me," he explained.

"What have you done?" God asked Eve.

"The snake told me to do it," Eve said, bursting into tears.

"You enticed Eve?" God asked the snake.

"Ssso what, ssso what," hissed the snake.

"It's just a sssilly sssnake joke."

But God was not in a laughing mood. "Since you did this," God said to the snake, "you will be cursed. You will have to crawl on the ground and eat dust for your entire life. People will step on you, and you will bite them. They will strike at your head, and you will strike at their heels."

"Who caresss," hissed the snake venomously as he slithered away.

"As for you," God turned to Adam and Eve, who were standing off to the side, frightened, "I will banish you from the Garden of Eden. You won't have fruit and animals and fish like in the Garden of Eden. You'll have to plow and plant and work the land by the sweat of your brow in order to have bread to eat."

He cast out Adam and Eve from the garden. And ever since then, people have worked hard for their food, and worn clothes, and dreamt that perhaps one day God will forgive us and permit us to return, once again, to the Garden of Eden.

Noah's Ark

Noah was a good and honest man. He had three sons. The oldest was Shem, the middle one was Ham, and the youngest was Yefet.

All the people on earth behaved terribly. They hit, lied, stole, and sometimes they even killed one another. God looked down from heaven at the people God had created and said, "What a shame that I created this world. I should never have bothered." God decided to bring a great flood that would wash everyone away.

Everyone, that is, except Noah, because Noah was a good and honest man. God told him to build a large ark that would have three stories, multiple cabins, a side door, and a window overhead.

"Does a family with three children really need such a gigantic ark?" Noah wondered.

"It's not just for you and your family," God explained. "It's for animals, too. Two of each kind will come aboard, male and female, so that the various animals will survive the flood as well."

Noah went to the forest, chopped down great big trees, and began building the ark. Soon, people started gathering around his house, making fun of him.

"What are you doing, Noah?"

"I'm building a big ark," he responded.

"You're going to live in a box?" they mocked him.

And Noah responded, "God is bringing a great flood. If you start behaving properly, God will forgive you, and you'll be saved."

"Flood, shmud," the people said. "What do we need to be saved from? A little rain?" They pointed their finger at him and teased, "Noah, Noah has no brain. Scared about a drop of rain."

When the ark was ready, the animals began to arrive from all over the land. Two by two, male and female: lion and lioness, horse and mare, rooster and hen. Spiders and ants and flies and worms. They all arrived in an orderly manner and lined up in front of the ark.

Noah opened the door and said, "Please come in, there's no need to push. There's enough room for everyone."

But God said,

"Hurry up, the flood is coming."

"Just a minute, God," Noah insisted. "We have to wait for the turtle and his wife."

The turtles arrived, Noah closed the door, and the flood began. The waters rose and lifted the ark until it began to float. The land could no longer be seen because it was covered in water, then the houses and the tall trees disappeared, and finally, even the tops of the mountains went under.

Noah stood by the window of the ark, looking out. Wherever he looked, all he could see was water. He and his family and the animals in the ark were the only creatures still alive—and the fish, who didn't mind the rain and water.

The ark was a happy place. Noah's family and all the animals enjoyed being together. But the days passed, and the flood didn't end, and it grew more crowded, and it started to get boring.

Noah said, "We need to wait patiently until the flood ends." But the days passed and the rain fell, and Noah began to think that maybe God had forgotten about them, and they would sail on forever, and would never be able to leave the ark.

But God did not forget about them.

After forty days, God brought the flood to an end, and the waters began to recede. They sank lower and lower until the tops of the mountains looked like islands, and the ark came to a stop atop Mount Ararat.

Everyone wanted to get out—to run around, to play, to go wild. But just to be safe, Noah took a dove in his palm and told her, "Fly away, dove. Go fly away and see. Have the waters receded from the surface of the earth?"

The dove flew out and then returned immediately. She found no dry land on which to rest.

A few days passed, and once again, Noah took the dove and told her,

**"Fly away, dove.
Go fly away and see.
Have the waters receded from
the surface of the earth?"**

This time the dove returned with an olive branch. And then Noah knew that the waters had gone down, and the tops of the trees were visible.

Noah waited a few more days, and then he sent the dove a third time. This time the dove did not return, and Noah understood that the waters had dried up.

He opened the ark, and everyone ventured out: ram and ewe, bull and cow, tiger and tigress, and a few little ones that had been born along the way. Everyone excitedly barked and bleated and bellowed and baaed.

Noah and his family were the last to emerge. They looked around and did not recognize what they saw. There were no people. It was only them, and the animals who had been with them on the ark, and the ark itself, which rested atop the mountain.

**Noah lifted his head
to thank God,**

and then he saw a colorful rainbow in the heavens. And ever since then, whenever we see a rainbow in the sky, we know that God will never bring a flood again. And when we want to draw a symbol of peace, we draw a dove with an olive branch, like the dove that brought the news to Noah that the flood was over at last.

The Tower of Babel

One day, a very long time ago, people sat looking up at the sky. They saw the sun and moon and a thousand stars, clouds drifting through the heavens, and birds flapping their wings. It seemed that the only ones not up there in the sky were people.

"How can we reach the heavens?" they asked one another. "We can't jump that high. We can't fly. What can we do?"

They sat and thought and made all sorts of suggestions, until one wise man stood up and said, "I know. Let's build a great tower with its top in the sky."

They dug deep foundations in the earth, prepared bricks, and began to build. Brick upon brick, brick upon brick. The tower rose higher and higher. In the beginning it was as tall as a tree, and then it was as tall as a large house, and then it was as tall as a mountain.

"Is this tall enough?" they wondered.

But others said, "No. A tower is not something you stop building. You keep building higher and higher, as high as you can."

And they built and built, and the tower nearly reached the clouds, but they didn't stop building. They built so high that they could no longer go up and down, and so they stayed at the top, and workers carried up more and more bricks. They built and built, higher and higher, and soon they couldn't see the birds anymore, and even the clouds were beneath them. No one remembered what they needed the tower for.

They just kept building.

When the angels in the sky looked down, they suddenly saw the tower getting taller and taller and closer and closer to them.

"Oh my," one of the angels said. "One of us is going to bump into that tower and get hurt tonight."

"And anyway," said another angel. "The heavens are not a place for people. People belong on earth."

"What shall we do?" the angels asked God.

"First of all, we have to let them build a little more, and then we'll decide," God said.

The people continued building, and the tower grew even taller, until it covered the clouds. The angels hurried to God and said, "The tower has already reached us in the middle of the heavens. We have to do something about it."

God peered down and saw the tower. It was enormous, with its top in the heavens.

"Who would have thought that these tiny creatures could build such a tower," said God. "I'm starting to think that they're capable of quite a lot."

"You have to destroy the tower," the angels cried out. "You have to kill all the people."

"There's no need to kill or destroy," said God. God smiled and said, "Maybe we will just confuse them, so that they can no longer understand one another." And just like that God waved a hand, and the people began speaking different languages.

Until that point, all the people on earth had spoken a single language and understood one another. But suddenly they began speaking many different languages: Hebrew, English, Inuit, Hungarian, Arabic, Russian, Chinese—and they no longer understood one another.

"Pass me the hammer," one builder said to another in Hebrew. But the second builder spoke only Hungarian, so he passed him a screwdriver instead. "Take this brick," another worker said in Italian. But his friend understood only Amharic, and he gave him a bucket instead. "Please mix the sand and the mortar," someone asked in Russian. But his friend understood only Japanese, and he climbed the ladder instead.

Then they began to get angry and to argue and to yell and to curse one another in every language. But they didn't even understand one another's curses, which only made them angrier. They began beating one another. All the builders ran down from the tower, and everyone searched for friends who could understand them.

All the English speakers went to one place, all the Chinese speakers to another, and all the Greek speakers to yet another place. And in that way everyone scattered and created their own nations.

And what happened to the tower?

The tower remained there alone and abandoned. At first the angels would play hide-and-seek in it, and birds built their nests inside, and parents would point it out to their children and say, "See that? It's forbidden to build such a tall tower, because God doesn't allow it."

Then the tower began to crumble. Rain fell on it, the sun beat down on it, the wind lashed at its walls, and then it collapsed, until it was no more. And today we do not even know where it once stood.

Abraham and Sarah

The first Jews, Abraham and Sarah, had everything a person could want. They had gold and silver, camels and cows, sheep and shepherds, fields and wells.

But Abraham and Sarah wanted something even more important. They wanted children. All their days they prayed to God to grant them a child—at least one.

Abraham was a good and honest man, and God loved him and promised to give him whatever he requested. But as the years passed, and as Abraham and Sarah grew older, they gave up hope of ever having a child.

One night God said to Abraham,

"Look up to the heavens and count the stars."

Abraham said, "The heavens are filled with stars. It is impossible to count them all."

"I will give you as many children as the number of stars that you see in the sky," said God. "You will have a son, and that son will have children, and those children will have more and more children until they will be as numerous as the stars in the sky."

Abraham remained silent and continued to look up at the heavens. He thought to himself that it would be enough to look at just one star. If God would grant him even just one son, that would be the most wonderful thing that ever happened to him.

The next day Abraham got up, sat outside, and waited to see if anyone would pass through the desert in need of food, or a place to rest. He waited and waited, but no one came. The morning hours had already passed, and the sun rose and blazed high in the sky.

Abraham remained outside waiting, in case he might be able to invite anyone in after all.

Sarah called out to him from inside the tent,

"Abraham, you're going to get a sunburn. Come inside."

But Abraham said, "If I come inside, I won't be able to see any travelers who might approach, and I won't be able to invite them in and host them."

Sarah sighed, because she knew that Abraham loved hosting guests, and nothing she could do or say would change that.

Abraham kept waiting. In the afternoon, he lifted his eyes and saw not one traveler, but three.

He ran toward them and said, "Come, dear travelers. You are surely tired and thirsty. Rest in the shade, eat and drink, and then you can continue your journey."

The people were very tired indeed. They sat down under the great oak tree, and Abraham went to the tent and said to his wife, "Sarah, hurry up. Our guests have arrived. Take some of our best flour and make them cakes."

He rushed to prepare a giant feast, and when they ate, he said to them, "Eat more, please, so you don't get hungry."

The guests ate and drank, and after the meal they asked Abraham, "Where is your wife, Sarah?"

"She's in the tent," Abraham responded. He was surprised at how the travelers, who had come from far away, knew that he had a wife and that her name was Sarah.

"Abraham," they said, "exactly one year from now, you and Sarah will have a son."

Sarah sat inside the tent and listened to the guests' words.

"Ha, ha, ha," she laughed out loud.

"What kind of talk is this? I'm going to have a child? At my age? Anyone who hears that will laugh at me," she said to herself.

The guests got up from their seats and said to Abraham, "Why did Sarah laugh at what we said? We're not ordinary men—we're angels of God. God sent us to tell you both that God has not forgotten the promise, and in another year you will have a son." Then the guests set out on their way. Abraham watched them until they disappeared from sight.

And indeed, exactly one year after the angels' visit, Abraham and Sarah had a son. They called him Isaac, meaning "he will laugh," because Sarah had said, "Anyone who hears this will laugh at me."

Isaac had a son named Jacob, and Jacob had twelve sons, and we—the children of Israel, as numerous as the stars in the sky—are descended from them, just as God promised Abraham.

Joseph and His Brothers

The patriarch Jacob had twelve sons: Reuven, Shimon, Levi, Judah, Dan, Naftali, Gad, Asher, Issachar, Zevulin, and the little ones, Joseph and Benjamin.

Of all his sons, Jacob loved Joseph the most. He would play with him, tell him stories, and make him toys.

When Joseph grew older, his father sewed him a striped coat. It was a wondrous coat made of delicate fabric with fine stripes. Joseph put it on and went outside so that everyone would see the new coat his father had given him.

When the brothers saw the striped coat, they grew very angry. Jacob hadn't made any of them a nice coat like that.

"Look what a beautiful coat my father sewed for me,"

Joseph bragged.

But his brothers ignored him.

"He sewed this coat for me alone," Joseph continued provoking his brothers. "Look how soft and fine the fabric is, with beautiful embroidered stripes . . ."

But the brothers just set off to herd their sheep.

The next day, Joseph came back, still wearing his striped coat. He returned to his brothers, who were shepherding their flocks in the field. "Greetings," he said to them. "I came back to visit."

They did not respond.

"Do you want to hear what I dreamed last night?" Joseph asked.

"No," the brothers responded in unison. "Get out of here with that coat of yours. You look silly."

"You're just jealous," Joseph said. "But I'm going to tell you anyway. I dreamed that we were all cutting wheat in the field. Then suddenly all your wheat stalks came and bowed down to mine."

The brothers were silent.

"Nice dream, right?" Joseph asked.

"You think we're going to bow down to you?" the brothers yelled. "Go home before we beat you, you piece of coat, you. Stupid stalk."

Joseph fled home, but the next day he returned wearing the striped coat and went down to the field.

"Greetings," he called to his brothers. "Here I am."

Again, the brothers ignored Joseph.

"I dreamed a dream tonight as well. Do you want to hear my new dream?"

"No!" the brothers cried out. "We have no use for your dreams."

"Tonight I dreamed," continued Joseph, "that the sun and moon and eleven stars came and bowed down to me."

This dream, too, infuriated Joseph's brothers. They tried to jump on him and beat him, but Joseph fled home.

The next day Joseph wore his coat again and went down to the pasture to visit his brothers.

"Here comes that dreamer,"

said Judah.

"I wonder what dream he's going to tell us about today," said Naftali.

"He's come to annoy us with his stupid stripes," yelled Zevulun and Yissachar.

"Let's catch him," cried Dan and Gad.

"Let's beat him," suggested Asher.

"It's not nice to beat someone—let's kill him instead," snarled Shimon and Levi, who were particularly angry.

All the brothers jumped on Joseph and caught hold of him. But Reuven, the oldest son, took pity on him. "Don't kill him," he said. "Let's go throw him into the pit."

"But we'll take his striped coat from him," the brothers insisted.

Joseph tried to grab hold of his coat. He cried out, "It's my coat—my striped coat that Father sewed for me!" But his older brothers ripped it off him and threw him into a pit in the field.

Joseph sat in the pit, the tears streaming down his cheeks. Meanwhile his brothers sat down to eat.

Suddenly they heard the sound of bells ringing in the distance. A caravan of Midianite merchants came by on their way to Egypt.

Judah said to his brothers, "Instead of leaving Joseph to die in the pit, let's sell him to the Midianites."

"Good thinking," cried Zevulun. "Then we won't need to deal with him and his stripes and his dreams."

The brothers threw ropes down into the pit,

pulled out Joseph, and sold him to the Midianites.

"You should be ashamed of yourselves," Joseph cried. "I'm your brother."

"We don't need a brother like you," the brothers mocked him.

"You should be happy we didn't kill you," said Shimon.

"I'm going to tell Father about all of this," Joseph wept.

"You'll never see him again," Levi responded.

"And you won't see your striped coat again either," Naftali said.

The Midianites took Joseph with them down to Egypt, and the brothers remained in the field. Slowly they began to understand what a terrible thing they had done, and they grew frightened.

"What will we do now?" they asked one another. "Father will ask where Joseph is . . . What will we tell him?"

They took the torn coat, dipped it in sheep's blood, returned home, and told their father, "We found this striped coat, stained with blood."

Joseph recognized the striped coat he had sewn for Joseph. He saw the blood and thought that a bear or a lion had killed his son.

"Joseph was torn apart by a beast! A savage beast devoured him!" he cried. He tore his clothes and wept.

But Joseph did not die. The Midianites brought him to Egypt and sold him to a wealthy man named Potiphar.

Joseph had many adventures in Egypt.

At first he was a servant in Potiphar's home, then he was placed in jail, and then one day he interpreted a dream for Pharaoh, king of Egypt, and he rose to glory.

This is all very important and all very interesting. But what is far more important and interesting is that after many years, Joseph and his brothers met again. And what is most important and interesting of all is that Joseph also met his father again—the patriarch Jacob—who was by that point already a very old man. But that is another story, for another time.

Moses in the River

For many years, the Israelites lived peacefully in Egypt until an evil king came to power. He was known as Pharaoh.

Pharaoh asked, "Who are these foreigners living in our country?"

His wise men answered him, "These are members of the family of Jacob and Joseph, who came to live in Egypt many years ago. They had numerous children and grandchildren, and now there are so many of them."

Pharaoh decided to turn all the Israelites into his slaves. He wanted them to build impressive cities, strong fortresses, and fancy palaces. He appointed his taskmasters and foremen over them with whips, and the Israelites groaned from all the backbreaking labor.

But for Pharaoh, it was still not enough. His evil heart continued to scheme. He said, "The Israelites may be my slaves, but they are already great and numerous, and soon they will outnumber us." He informed all the Egyptians, "Every Israelite boy that is born must be thrown into the Nile River."

At the time there was an Israelite woman living in Egypt known as Yocheved. She gave birth to a son—a sweet and lovely boy. All the members of the family looked at him, but instead of smiling, they burst out in tears: "Soon the Egyptians will come and take our baby. They will throw him into the river and he'll drown."

And Yocheved said, "We won't tell anyone that he was born.

We'll hide him at home."

But it was very hard to hide a baby at home. Sometimes an Egyptian neighbor would come in and say, "Was that a baby I just heard crying?"

And then they would have to make up all sorts of stories—it wasn't a baby, but a wailing cat or a creaky door.

After three months had passed, Yocheved said, "We can't hide our baby anymore." Moses's big sister Miriam said, "But the Egyptians will throw him into the river . . ."

Yocheved thought and thought, and finally she said, "I know what we can do."

She made a small basket out of wicker, and she covered it with tar so the water would not enter inside. She spread a thin blanket inside the ark and placed the baby on it, covering him with a sheet.

"We'll let our baby float in the river.

Perhaps someone will have mercy on him and rescue him," Yocheved said. She and Miriam took the basket and placed it in the river, among the reeds.

Yocheved returned home. She could not bear to stay and watch the basket with her baby float down the river. "Protect my son," she prayed to God. "Don't let him die."

Miriam hid among the reeds and said, "I'll stay here and watch over my little brother from a distance."

That day it was particularly hot in Egypt, and the daughter of Pharaoh went down to bathe in the river. Suddenly she caught sight of a small basket floating toward her in the river. She was curious to see what was inside.

"Take that basket out of the water," she instructed her maidservant.

Her maidservant brought the basket to her. Pharaoh's daughter took off the cover and saw a handsome little baby asleep inside.

Pharaoh's daughter was not evil like her father. She took pity on the baby and said to herself, "This is surely an Israelite baby, one my father wanted to kill. What should I do now?"

Then Miriam emerged from her hiding place, approached Pharaoh's daughter, and said to her, "If you'd like, I can bring a woman who could nurse this boy. He's surely very hungry."

Pharaoh's daughter agreed, and Miriam ran home as fast as her legs could carry her, until she reached her mother, Yocheved. She said to her mother, "Come immediately. Pharaoh's daughter found our baby, and she wants someone to come nurse him."

Pharaoh's daughter did not know that the nursemaid was the baby's mother. She said to Yocheved, "Take this child and raise him for me until he is weaned. Then bring him to the palace, and he will be my son."

The whole family was very happy. Now they didn't have to hide the baby from anyone anymore. If their Egyptian neighbors stopped by to ask, "Who is that baby in your house?" they responded, "This is Pharaoh's daughter's baby. We are raising him for her until he finishes nursing."

And indeed, when the baby grew a bit older, Yocheved brought him to the king's palace and gave him to Pharaoh's daughter. She was very sad, but she also knew that he would not be cast into the river or forced to become a slave like the Israelites in Egypt.

Pharaoh's daughter loved the boy very much. She called him Moses, which means "drawn," because he was drawn from the river. Moses lived in Pharaoh's home until he became a young man. It was then that he realized that he was not an Egyptian, but an Israelite. He left Pharaoh's palace and became a shepherd in the wilderness, and when he returned,

he freed all of his nation's people from slavery.

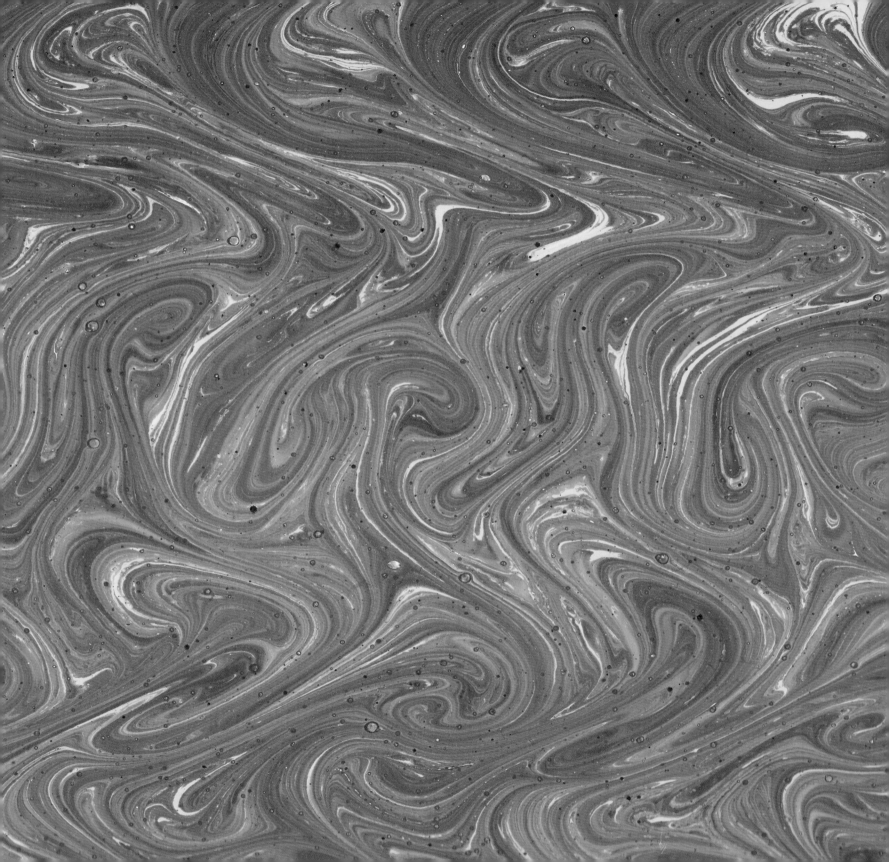